# Also an OCTOPUS

or

A LITTLE BIT OF NOTHING

MAGGIE TOKUDA-HALL

illustrated by

BENJI DAVIES

CANDLEWICK PRESS

Every story starts the same way . . .

with nothing. ———————————————————→

And every story needs a character.
Any character you can imagine!

Like a little girl.

Or an adorable bunny.

Or better yet . . .

# AN OCTOPUS!

An octopus who plays the ukulele.

But in order for it to be a story,
and not just an octopus,
that octopus needs to want something.

Like a sandwich.

Or a friend.

Or a totally awesome shining purple spaceship capable of intergalactic travel.

But that ukulele-playing octopus with intergalactic dreams can't just GET a shining purple spaceship, from, say, the drugstore.

And just why not?

That would be silly.

No, *you're* silly.

And also, that would make for a very short, very dull story.

For the story to be as totally awesome as a purple spaceship, the octopus has to earn it, by, say . . .

But what if the spaceship doesn't work?

THEN the octopus will try again,
but this time, with some help.

From an adorable bunny.

Ta-da!

Bunnies, while good friends, are not rocket scientists.

Not usually, anyway.

So the totally awesome spaceship
isn't totally awesome yet,
and it's certainly not capable
of intergalactic travel.

It's just a big mess.

Thanks anyway,
chum.

By now, the octopus is starting to give up.

The octopus feels heartbroken.

As if the octopus will *never, ever* get on
a totally awesome shining purple spaceship
and fly to other galaxies.

So the octopus plays the ukulele,
because music is good for the heart.

But as the octopus plays, a strange thing happens:
the resolution to the story begins to take shape.

People come to listen to the
ukulele-playing octopus.

Friends. Strangers. Lots of people.

And a FEW of those people?
They're rocket scientists.

Rocket scientists who don't just
build rocket ships — they also play
the saxophone, tambourine,
trumpet, and lute!

So what happens next?

That's up to you.

When one story ends, it's just making room
for another story to begin.

And whether it's a story about a little girl,
an adorable bunny, an octopus,
rocket scientists, or a band,
you've already got what it takes
to make that story whole.

Because every story starts
with the same thing:

just a little bit of nothing.

And everyone has a little bit of nothing!

It's true!

To my grandparents, storytellers all
M. T. H.


For Kasper and Lilly
B. D.

First edition 2016

Library of Congress Catalog Card Number 2015937118
ISBN 978-0-7636-7084-9

16 17 18 19 20 21 CCP 10 9 8 7 6 5 4 3 2 1

Printed in Shenzhen, Guangdong, China

MIX
Paper from
responsible sources
FSC® C008047

This book was typeset in Agenda Medium.
The illustrations were created digitally.

Candlewick Press
99 Dover Street
Somerville, Massachusetts 02144

visit us at www.candlewick.com

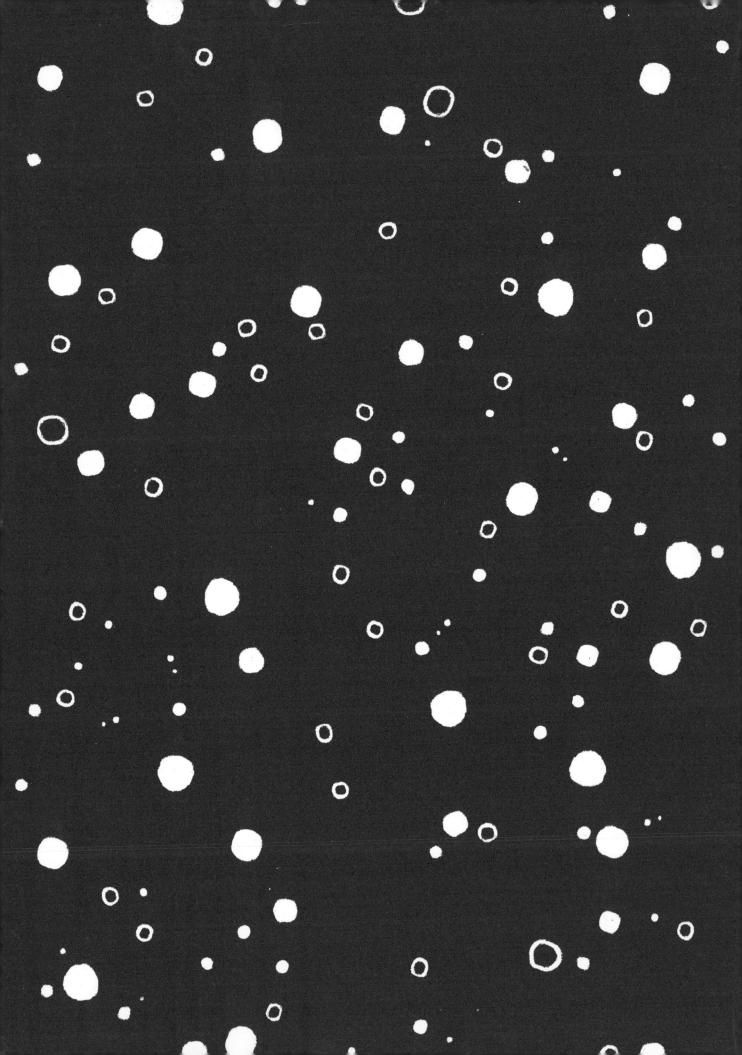